Tales of Transformation

Kenneth Haines

Tales of Transformation - Series One

Published by Spines Publishing Platform

ISBN: 979-8-89691-505-8

Tales of Transformation

Series One

Kenneth Haines

Contents

The Slave Child

The Secrets of Rosie

The Orphanage Child

The Slave Child

SLAVE CHILD

Chapter 1
Liyanah

IT'S BEEN three years since Liyanah was sold to a slave dealer. She turned into a emotionless, quiet, and obedient slave, but her youth made her less appealing to the customers.

The slave dealer grew increasingly concerned. He was unsure of how to handle her as she didn't seem attractive to the buyers. The slave dealer was flogging and venting his anger at her again today. That's when I stepped in and stopped his assault.

The slave dealer stopped flogging and instantly said, "Offering her cheaply."

"Please buy me!" Liyanah said.

"Hmm," I hesitated. (His night is already fulfilled with his mature maids, so why does he need the tiny slave for?) After a long pause, I looked into her eyes and bought her from the slave dealer at a bargain price. I dragged Liyanah's leash and headed to my great mansion.

She was overwhelmed by the enormous mansion, she had never seen in her life. I take her to a cramped barn behind the mansion. The barn was full of shambles. There didn't seem to be enough room for her to lie down here. Now this was Liyanah's residence.

"Stay here, I'll be back for you," I was being mean at that moment, not knowing what to say exactly.

Liyanah obediently curled up in a corner of the tiny barn, waiting for her owner's return. She didn't bother to ask where he was going and what he was doing; she had learned long ago not to question her master's orders, no matter how cruel or inhuman they might seem.

She could hear me coming for her, I slammed the door open, walked over to her, and ordered her to get up. “Stand up and come here, child!!”

Hearing the door slamming open, Liyanah slowly rose to her feet, her heart pounding in fear. As her Master approached her, she forced herself to remain standing straight, her head bowed submissively.

"Please don't beat me... I'll do anything you want," she whispered, taking a small step forward.

She saw me reaching for her neck with both my hands, she closed her eyes waiting for the worst to come).

“Hold still, child.” Liyanah trembled as her master's hand reached for her neck.

She knew what he was going to do, but she couldn't move. She had been conditioned since childhood to obey without question, no matter how much pain it brought her. Her mind was filled with pleading thoughts, begging for him to show mercy.

(I unclasp her collar, and she hears it hit the floor with a loud thud. In a calmer voice, she heard me) “No child of mine will ever be treated like this again!”

Relief washed over Liyanah as the collar fell from her neck, but she remained rigid and silent. She couldn't comprehend Master Haines's sudden change of heart. All she knew was to be grateful and comply with whatever he demanded.

"T-Thank you, Master," she murmured softly, her eyes still cast down. (I lifted her in my arms and carried her to the house).

Liyanah was too scared to move as her Master lifted her up in his arms and carried her into the house. She had no idea what was happening or what his intentions were. All she could do was hope that this new kindness wouldn't be short-lived and that she would be able to earn her master's approval finally.

(I carried her to a long hall that was not lit well and shadows danced everywhere along the walls, we came to a big door)

Liyanah shivered as her Master carried her through the dimly lit hallway, her heart racing with fear and anticipation. She didn't dare to ask where they were going or what was happening. All she could do was cling to the hope that this was somehow a test of her loyalty and obedience. "M-Master?" she whispered, her voice trembling slightly.

"W-What's happening?"

“Shhh, child.” Liyanah bit her lip and nodded silently, trying to suppress her fear and anxiety. She didn't want to displease her Master or risk another beating.

"I'm sorry, Master," she whispered, her eyes downcast. "I'll be quiet."

“It's ok, I didn't mean to scare you.” (I silently opened the door and she could smell the aroma in the air as I carried her in. Gently, I helped her to her feet and guided her to a stool. As she sat down, her eyes darted around. She was taking in the surroundings, especially the bathroom with a tub overflowing with bubbles).

“Sit there please so I can show you things around.”

Liyanah's heart raced as her Master carried her into the luxurious bathroom. The scent of sweet-smelling soap and warm water filled her senses. She couldn't help but feel a strange mixture of curiosity and apprehension. She did as she was told, sitting down on the stool by the tub and looking up at him nervously.

"Yes, Master?" she asked softly, her eyes full of questions.

“Okay my dear, whatever I'll be showing you, you must remember it, this is your bathroom.”

Liyanah listened carefully, trying to commit every detail to memory. A bathtub filled with warm water and soft, sudsy bubbles, scented candles flickering on the marble ledge beside the tub, and elegant towels neatly folded on a stack near the sink.

"Yes, Master," she repeated obediently. "I'll remember everything."

“Good girl. Now the most important part. No more calling me ‘master’. Call me Pops instead. You’re the only one in this house who is allowed to call me that.

Liyanah's eyes widened in surprise at the Master's request. She had never addressed her Master with a nickname before, especially not one, so personal and intimate. However, she knew better than to question his orders.

"Yes, Pops," she replied softly, practicing the new name in her mind. "I won't forget."

"I'm no longer your master, dear. I free you from your bondage, you are given a new life here. In this household, the servants and maids will recognize you as my daughter. They will treat you with respect, and you will do the same for them. I'll leave you now to freshen up. Take your time and if you can rediscover the little girl who once lived in here." (Pointing to her heart).

Liyanah's heart was racing as Pop's spoke. She couldn't believe he was giving her freedom and treating her like a daughter. It was a far cry from the abuse and neglect she had endured in the past.

"Thank you, Pops," she whispered, her voice shaking with emotion. "I promise I'll make you proud."

"Ok, dear. Oh, don't forget to wash behind your ears." (I left the bathroom giving her privacy and closed the door and went across the hall and got her room ready for her).

Liyanah blushed at Pops instruction, but she knew she had to follow it if she wanted to please him. She took a deep breath and began untying the knot on the back of her dress, letting it slide off her shoulders. She hesitated for a moment before stepping into the warm, bubbly water, letting out a soft sigh of relief.

As she washed herself, she tried to imagine what it would be like to be truly free and loved, but the memories of her past abuse were still fresh in her mind. She promised herself that she would try her best to be the perfect daughter for Pops, even if it meant sacrificing some of her own desires and wants.

When she finally stepped out of the tub, her skin glowing with the scent of lavender. She found Pops waiting for her in the bedroom. He had transformed the room into a cozy little nook just for her, with soft pillows, a warm blanket, and a frilly nightgown laid out on the bed.

"It's beautiful, Pops," she said, her voice filled with awe. "Thank you so much."

“Oh, dear, you like your room and how about being my daughter?” Liyanah's heart swelled with gratitude as she looked around her new room. She couldn't believe Pops had gone to such great lengths to make her feel welcome and loved. As for being his daughter, she knew it was just a role she was playing, but she also couldn't deny the strange sense of comfort and belonging it brought her.

"Yes, Pops," she replied softly, a small smile tugging at the corners of her lips. "I'm happy to be your daughter."

“Honey, it's not a role, tomorrow I'll be getting it legal that you are my daughter so no one can question it.” (I picked her up into my arms and tightly hugged her and kissed her forehead.)

Liyanah gasped out softly as Master Haines scooped her up into his arms, holding her close., the warmth of being wanted and cared for in such a way seemed unbelievable to her. His mention of making things official stirred deep emotions within her but she managed to reciprocate with a smile.

"Thank you, Pops," she whispered, resting her head against his chest. "I'm glad I'm not dreaming."

“Now it's late. Get some sleep, we have a big day tomorrow. If you need me, I'm in the next room by yours, now hop in bed, honey.” (I covered up and tucked her in lightly kissed her forehead and went to my room)

“Good night, dear. Love you!”

Liyanah snuggled deeper into her warm blanket, feeling the weariness from the day finally catching up to her. As Master Haines kissed her gently on the forehead, she felt a strange mix of fear and excitement bubbling up inside her. But she forced herself to relax and focus on the feeling of safety and security that he provided.

"Good night, Pops," she whispered softly, closing her eyes and allowing herself to drift off to sleep.

Chapter 2
New Beginning

THE NEXT MORNING, I walked into her room and bent down and kissed her forehead.

“Time to get up little one.” That arduous moment just before throwing an utterance when I glanced at her face, all I could see were innumerable unanswered questions written all over it. How unfortunate that reading her face was uncomplicated and yet seemed futile to give it a thought.

Liyanah stirred in her bed, groaning softly as the morning sun streamed through the window. She didn't want to leave the warmth and comfort of her bed, but the sound of Pop's voice made her open her eyes. "Okay, Pop's," she said, sitting up and rubbing the sleep from her eyes. "What plans do you have for today?"

“Just relax and sit there. Enjoy the morning air and sun shine on you, There's no hurry getting out of bed.”

(She looks energetic and smells a lot better than when I brought her home) Liyanah nodded obediently and opened the curtains wider, letting the warm sunshine fill the room. She took a deep breath and closed her eyes, trying to embrace the moment and forget about her worries.

"Thank you, Pops," she whispered.

“You look very pretty in that nightgown. It suits you well! I didn't know it would fit you perfectly.”

Liyanah blushed slightly, looking down at the frilly nightgown she was wearing. “It was one of my daughter's favorites,” He insisted she wear it for him. It brought back good memories.

"Thank you, Pops," she replied softly, keeping her eyes lowered.

(She sat back on her bed, leaning against the headboard, having her legs up like she was ready to hop and I could see everything underneath her nightgown) Liyanah bit her lower lip, feeling exposed and vulnerable with Pop's gaze on her. She was surprised by the warmth in his voice and the way he looked at her. Despite her initial fears, she found herself starting to trust him more.

"Thank you, Pops," she whispered, trying to maintain her composure. "I'm glad you're happy with me."

“I'm very happy with you darling, more than you will ever realize.”

Liyanah swallowed hard, feeling a mix of emotions churning inside her. She wanted to believe him, to trust him, but old habits die hard. She forced herself to meet his gaze, trying to show him that she was loyal and obedient.

"I'll do my best to make you happy, Pops," she said softly.

(She looked scared and the fear as I got down in front of her and was coming closer to the space between her legs. I grabbed her ankles tenderly, lowered her legs, adjusted her nightgown, and again kissed her forehead).

“You need to respect yourself, dear. I just want you to know I love you and never forget that.”

Liyanah sighed in relief when Pop's touch turned out to be gentle and affectionate. She struggled to find the words to express how she felt about him. Her heart hammering in her chest was loud and eminently audible. Even though she didn't fully understand the concept of love, she knew she didn't want to disappoint him.

"Thank you, Pops," she managed to say. "I love you too."

You hear that the Maids and servants have arrived, "Come here child.” (She got off the bed and saw a box on the floor, inside was a pink beautiful silk dress and pink panties)

“Here put this on, I want my daughter to look like a princess when she meets her staff.”

Liyanah nodded obediently, her heart racing at the thought of meeting the other servants. She carefully picked up the silky dress and panties, feeling the softness between her fingers. She stepped into the dressing room, taking her time to change into the elegant attire.

"Thank you, Pops," she muttered, coming back out to show him how she looked.

"You need to remember you are no longer a servant or a piece of property, you are Liyana Haines, Daughter to Count Drake Haines, always remember that, darling. That's you from now on."

Liyanah looked up at Pops with a mix of awe and uncertainty. His words were heavy, filling her with both joy and anxiety. She couldn't believe he wanted her to be his daughter. Suddenly, she felt an intense surge of loyalty and protectiveness towards him.

"Yes, Pops," she said quietly. "I'll always remember."

"Come here, child." (I held her tightly against me and knelt down). "Darling, I love you and as long as I'm alive, I will make sure you're respected and loved like you've never been before."

Liyanah felt her eyes mist over as Master Haines called her his daughter and expressed his love for her.

She had never known anything like this before, but somehow it felt right. She wrapped her arms around his waist, holding on tight as if she was afraid to lose him.

"I love you too, Pops," Her tears uncontrollably fell off her face while she gripped him tight. "Thank you for everything."

"I was wondering how you'd feel calling me dad or daddy when surrounded with people. My friends call me Pops but you are more than a friend to me, you're my daughter now."

Liyanah blushed deeply at the thought of calling pops 'dad' or 'daddy' in front of others. She knew it was a sign of affection and loyalty, but it still made her feel self-conscious. She looked up at him with wide eyes, hoping he understood how much this all meant to her.

"I... I would be honored to call you 'dad' or 'daddy'," she said softly. "And I'm so grateful to have you in my life."

(We walked down the hall to the main room, holding hands while the staff stood in a row, their gazes fixed on her) "Everyone", I said. "Please meet Liyana, Princess Liyana.

She is now my daughter and I expect you to respect her and care for her as you would your own child." (They all stood at attention and knelt in acknowledgment) "Now please return to your duties."

Liyanah squeezed Pop's hand tightly, feeling both terrified and elated as he introduced her as his daughter to the rest of the staff. She could feel their stares boring into her back, making her heart race even faster.

But when Master Haines spoke kindly about her and made it clear he expected nothing less than the highest respect for his daughter, she straightened up her spine, her eyes fixed on a spot near the ceiling.

"Yes, Pops," she replied softly, her voice surprisingly firm. "Thank you, everyone." (me and Liyana went outside and sat on a swing to talk)

"So, darling how do you feel in here (pointing to her heart) about your new life and the freedom of never being a servant or slave again?"

Liyanah took a deep breath, still trying to process everything that had just taken a turn. She looked up at Master Haines with a mix of gratitude and confusion.

"I'm... I'm still getting used to it, Pops," I mean Dad. she said truthfully. "But I'm so grateful for your kindness and trust. I promise I won't let you down."

Liyanah smiled shyly as she thought about calling him 'dad' or 'daddy'. She knew it would be a big step for her, but she was ready. She took a deep breath and squeezed his hand tightly, her determination clear on her face.

"Okay, I'll try," she promised. "Pardon me if it takes time to get used to it."

"It's completely fine, dear. Now you have all the time." (I grabbed her hand gently and continued…)

"Would you answer me if I want to know something personal?"

"Of course, Daddy. You can ask me anything."

"What happened to your real parents and how did you end up being a slave?"

Liyanah bit her lower lip, her eyes fixed on a distant point. She hadn't spoken much about her past with anyone, and she felt nervous as she prepared to share this piece of her story with him.

"I was born into a poor family, Daddy," she began, her voice barely above a whisper.

"When I was five, my village was attacked by slavers. They... they killed everyone except me. They took me away and put me up for sale. No one bought me until the slave dealer got hold of me... He was a cruel man. He sold me to a lot of different owners. None of them were any kinder than he was. They used me as they wished... and eventually..."

Liyanah stopped, feeling a hot wave of shame and regret washed over her. Tears fell down her little cheeks. She couldn't continue telling him about the rest of the part. All she knew was that it had led her here, to this moment with Count Drake Haines.

“I'm sorry child for your loss and the treatment others did to you, extremely sorry.” Tears welled up in my eyes.

“Don't cry, Daddy.” (She hugged me and we both cried together).

“Look at you, now a princess!” (She got off the swing and spun around her beautiful dress swirling around with her). Liyanah smiled, feeling a little embarrassed but also happy that he saw her as a princess. She had always dreamed of being treated like one, even if it was just in her own mind.

"Thank you, Daddy," she said softly, looking up at him with gratitude in her eyes. "You're very kind to me."

“Honey, I don't say you’re a princess to make you feel good. That is your title from now on you will be known as Princess Liyana Haines since you are my daughter.” Liyanah's eyes widened in surprise as she heard him call her ‘Princess Liyana Haines'. It was the first time anyone had ever given her a title like that, and it felt strange but also kind of nice. She bowed her head slightly, a small smile playing on her lips.

"Thank you, Daddy," she repeated, her voice barely above a whisper. "I will try my best to live up to that title."

“You better. You are carrying a lot on these little shoulders, and from now on you walk proud of who you are.” (I reassured her about herself as her new identity).

“Yes, Daddy. I will do my best.” Liyana uttered quietly, her tone was promising and confident.

“Can dad get a big hug from his daughter?” She ran into my arms and gave me the biggest hug ever and I lifted her above my head and swirled her around with a joyful grin. Gently, I brought her down and wrapped her in an inseparable embrace.

Chapter 3
From Chains to Crown

SHE WAS THINKING about her life living free with servants her becoming a princess to her new dad and going to visit the village where it all started and seeing that horrible man that had her chained with a collar and was flogging her?

Today was the day she would return to the village, not as a slave, but as a princess. Word of her father's arrival spread rapidly through the villagers. As the horse-drawn carriage galloped into town, the villagers paused their activities, eyes fixed on the approaching vehicle.

The carriage door opened, and Lord Drake Haines stepped out, his presence commanding immediate attention. A small hand appeared next, and he gently helped his daughter down. The villagers gasped as they recognized her.

"This is my daughter, Princess Lilyana Haines," Lord Drake announced proudly.

"Is that...?" whispered one. "It can't be," murmured another. Lilyana felt a mix of emotions as she met the villagers' eyes—some filled with awe, others with skepticism. She stood tall, determined to embrace her new identity.

The Elder: A wise and respected figure in the village who remembers Liyanah from her past. They might be skeptical of her new status but eventually come to see her as a beacon of hope.

Just then, an elderly man approached them. His eyes, through clouded with age, held a sharpness that spoke of wisdom and experience. He wore simple, yet clean robes, and carried a staff that seemed more for tradition than necessity.

Liyanah's father stepped forward, extending his hand. "Elder, it is good to see you again. We have returned to help the village." The Elder hesitated for a moment, then clasped the offered hand firmly.

"We have heard of your new status. Many here are skeptical, but I see hope in your eyes. Perhaps you can bring the change we so desperately need."

Liyanah smiled, feeling a sense of purpose swell within her. "We will do our best, Elder. Together, we can make this village thrive again."

Flashbacks of Liyanah's past experiences with the slave dealer. the depth of her trauma and the significance of her return. Again she thought she saw him lurking in the shadows, a phantom of her past.

Fear rose up inside her, threatening to overwhelm her resolve. But she took a deep breath, grounding herself in the present. She was no longer that frightened child; she was a princess, determined to bring hope and change to her people.

Her father noticed the flicker of fear in her eyes and placed a reassuring hand on her shoulder. "You are strong, Liyanah. Together, we will overcome the shadows of the past." Liyanah nodded, drawing strength from his words. She turned back to the Elder, her voice steady. "We will not let fear hold us back. This village will thrive again."

Chapter 4
Confrontation to the Slave Dealer

As she lived under her new father's care, Princess Lilyana grappled with memories of her painful past. The opulence of her new life often clashed with the haunting recollections of her days in chains. Returning to the village where she had suffered, she felt a storm of emotions brewing within her.

The villagers watched in silence as she approached the man who had once held her captive. His eyes widened in recognition, but he quickly masked his fear with a sneer.

He mocked, "I see you've found a new life."

Lilyana's heart pounded. She could feel the weight of her past pressing down on her, but she stood tall.

"I have," she replied, her voice steady. "And I've come to ensure no one else suffers as I did."

The villagers murmured among themselves, their eyes darting between Lilyana and the man. Some looked at her with newfound respect, while others remained skeptical.

As days passed, Lilyana worked tirelessly to bring justice and healing to the village. She listened to the villagers' stories, offering support and seeking ways to make amends for the past. Yet, every night, she was haunted by the decision she knew she had to make.

Hints of her internal struggle began to surface in her actions. She would pause before passing judgment, Her eyes reflecting the turmoil within. She sought counsel from her father, Lord Drake, who advised her to follow her heart.

In quiet moments, she would visit the old, abandoned shack where she had once been held. There, she would sit in silence, grappling with the memories and the choices before her.

Would she seek vengeance or forgiveness? Justice or mercy? The villagers watched, waiting to see what kind of princess she would become.

In historical contexts, punishments during the time of kings and queens were often severe and publicly visible. Here are some fitting options for justice:

Justice for the Slave dealer

Public Flogging: The man could be publicly flogged in the village square. This would serve as both punishment and a warning to others.

Stocks or Pillory: He could be placed in stocks or a pillory, where villagers could throw rotten food or other objects at him. This humiliation was a common form of punishment.

Branding: Branding with a hot iron—perhaps on his hand or forehead—would permanently mark him as a wrongdoer.

Exile: Banishing him from the village or kingdom would ensure he never mistreats anyone again.

As they walked through the village, the young princess and her father took in the sight of the run-down huts, their thatched roofs sagging under the weight of neglect.

The air was thick with the earthy scent of freshly tilled soil and the faint aroma of cooking fires. Farmers, their hands calloused and faces weathered by the sun, bustled about, exchanging goods in a lively barter system.

A woman with a basket of eggs traded with a man offering a bundle of firewood, their transaction sealed with a nod and a smile. Nearby, a child held up a handful of herbs, hoping to trade for a loaf of bread. The princess noticed how the villagers' clothes were patched and worn, yet their spirits seemed unbroken.

Her father paused, his gaze sweeping over the scene. "This village has potential," he murmured, more to himself than to her. "But it needs so much more."

The princess nodded, her heart heavy with the realization of the work ahead. "We can help them, Father. We must."

A small child, around the princess's age, approached a vendor with a handful of herbs. Her eyes were wide with hope as she held them up. "Please, sir, can I trade these for some bread? My family hasn't eaten today."

The vendor, a kind-faced man with a bushy beard, looked down at the herbs and then at the child.

"These are good herbs, little one. I'll give you a loaf of bread for them."

The princess watched the exchange, her heart aching for the child's plight. She turned to her father, her voice soft but determined. "Father, we must help them. This village needs so much more."

Her father nodded, his gaze sweeping over the scene. "Yes, my dear. We will do everything we can."

As the days turned into weeks, Princess Lilyana's presence began to transform the village. Yet, the shadow of her past loomed large, and the villagers could sense her inner conflict.

One evening, as the sun dipped below the horizon, casting a golden glow over the village, Lilyana stood before the villagers. Her father, Lord Drake, stood beside her, offering silent support.

"I know many of you remember me as the girl in chains," she began, her voice steady but filled with emotion. "But there is one matter that remains unresolved." Her gaze shifted to the man who had once been her captor. He stood at the edge of the crowd, his expression unreadable.

"Justice must be served," she said, her voice firm. "But justice is not always about punishment. It is about healing and ensuring that such suffering never happens again."

The villagers held their breath, waiting to see what she would do next. Lilyana took a deep breath, her eyes meeting those of her former captor. Disgust flickered across her face, but she didn't say a word.

The villagers stood there, dwelling on what she might do. She turned away, her expression unreadable, and walked to her father. Grabbing his hand tightly, they walked outside together, leaving the villagers in a state of uncertainty and anticipation.

As the story neared its end, the tension in the village was palpable. The villagers had watched Princess Lilyana transform their lives, but the question of her former captor's fate still hung in the air.

On the day of the final judgment, the entire village gathered in the square. Lilyana stood before them, her father by her side, her expression resolute.

"Today, we close a chapter of pain and open one of hope," she began, her voice carrying the weight of her journey. "The man who once held me in chains will face his punishment."

The villagers leaned in, their breaths held in anticipation.

"Exile," she declared, her voice unwavering. "He will be banished from this village and kingdom, ensuring he never mistreats anyone again. And let it be known that never again shall any human—man, woman, or child—be in chains."

The villagers erupted in a mix of relief and applause. Lilyana's decision was both just and merciful, reflecting her growth and the lessons she had learned.

As her former captor was led away, Lilyana felt a sense of closure. She had faced her past and emerged stronger, ready to lead her people into a brighter future. The End

The Secrets of Rosie

Secrets of
Rosie

Chapter 1
Rosie

You moved into the eerie, dark house that belonged to your grandmother. The air was thick with the scent of old wood and forgotten memories. The house creaked and groaned, as if it were alive, whispering secrets through its walls.

Your grandmother had a list of peculiar house rules, but the one that stood out the most was her stern warning: "**Never open the last door at the end of the hall upstairs**." She never explained why, and her eyes would cloud over with a mix of fear and sadness whenever you asked.

Being a curious child, the forbidden door became an obsession. What could be behind it? Why was it never to be opened? Each night, as the house settled into its eerie silence, you found yourself drawn to the door, the mystery gnawing at your mind.

I woke up at midnight, thirsty. Something felt strange as I walked to the bathroom to get a drink of water, The door was calling me, not in words to my ears but inside my head.

Fear was creeping up inside me. I crept to the door and found it unlocked, its never was unlocked before, I turned the knob and the door creaked open. My heart was pumping in my chest as I slipped into the room and gently closed the creaking door.

I had to get adjusted to the darkness and only light shown in the room was the full moon shining in through the dusty dirty window glass. Shadows danced across the floor, and the air felt colder, almost as if the room itself was holding its breath.

As my eyes adjusted, I could make out the faint outlines of old furniture covered in white sheets, like ghosts frozen in time. The room smelled of mildew and something else, something eerie. I took a cautious step forward, the floorboards groaning under my weight.

There, sitting in a dusty rocker, was a girl doll, all covered with dust and webs. Slowly, I moved her hair from her face, revealing a blank stare. Her clothes were from another time period. She wore a dark blue dress and white stockings. The top part of her dress was supposed to be white ruffles, but with all the dust and webs, it looked faded, and the dress was the same way.

As I brushed away the cobwebs, a chill ran down my spine. The doll's eyes seemed to follow me, even though they were just painted glass. I couldn't shake the feeling that I was being watched. The room felt colder, and the silence was deafening.

I took a step back, my heart pounding in my chest. What was this doll doing here? Why had my grandmother forbidden me from entering this room? Questions swirled in my mind as I stood there, frozen in place, unable to tear my eyes away from the doll.

The next morning, after breakfast, I waited until my parents went to work before I approached Grandma about the room. I could see the fear in her eyes as I mentioned it. She took me by the hand, her grip trembling, and led me outside to the back porch.

We sat down, and she listened intently as I recounted what had happened the previous night and what I had seen. Her face grew paler with each word. When I finished, she took a deep breath, her voice shaky.

"Did you touch the doll or move the rocker?" she asked, her eyes wide with fear. I shook my head, sensing the gravity of her question. "No, Grandma, I didn't touch anything."

She sighed in relief, but the fear didn't leave her eyes. "That doll… it belonged to your great great-aunt. She… she died when she was just a child. The room has been locked ever since. There's something about that doll… something not right."

She mention that the dolls name was Rosie and it must never be taken from her rocking chair… then she asked if I closed the room back up and I told her I did, but I told her I couldn't lock the door for I didn't have a key. I can tell she is still very shaky and she said she needed to lay down.

That afternoon it started raining and getting windy and while I was in my room upstairs I started hearing banging and opened my door and followed the noise to the forbidden room.

Slowly I opened the door and saw that one of the old shudders was banging against the window. I opened the window almost didn't get it opened since its been closed for so many years.

These windows didn't open like today's windows; they opened inward like doors. Just as I opened it, a gust of wind blew in, knocking me aside and toppling the rocking chair.

Seeing the doll Rosie sprawled on the floor, I hurried to fix her rocker. Gently, I picked her up and placed her back in the chair.

I then went back to the window, secured the shutter, and closed the window. As I turned back, I sat down, staring at the now empty rocker, my heart pounding in my chest.

I walked out of that room and looked both ways to see if the doll was blown out of the room, not seeing anything I headed down the hall. I glance into the bathroom at there was Rosie sitting on the floor by the tub.

"How in the world did you get all the way down here?" I said muttered under my breath to myself. I gently picked her up and brought her back to her rocking chair and sat her down, I straightened her dress and I sat down on the dusty bed. my mind racing with questions.

I could feel her staring at me after I sat down on the bed. Her eyes, like any doll's, were cold and unmoving. But I knew something wasn't right. I swear I saw her move. Then, she spoke for the first time. Her voice was quiet but harsh, and her broken English sent chills down my spine.

"DDDon't move me again." She looked up at me, her eyes no longer empty. They were filled with anger and resentment.

"You are not to touch me. I am not a toy to be moved around as you please. I deserve to be treated with respect."

I stammered, "I'm sorry, I didn't know. I moved you from the bathroom thinking the wind blew you down the hall. I put you back in your chair safely. I didn't treat you wrong. I respected you and even straightened out your dress so you looked presentable."

Her eyes bore into mine, and for a moment, I thought I saw a flicker of understanding. But the anger remained, and I realized that this doll, Rosie, was more than just a toy. She had a story, a past, and perhaps a reason for her resentment.

"You have no idea what it is like to be treated as an object. I don't care about your 'respect' or your 'gentle' ways. I have been forced to stay in this rocking chair, to never leave ,for as long as I can remember.

My whole life has been nothing but a prisoner to that chair, and you have the audacity to tell me that I should be grateful?"

Her words cut deep, and I could feel the weight of her anger and pain. I took a deep breath, trying to find the right words to say. "I'm truly sorry, Rosie. I didn't know. I can't imagine what you've been through. But maybe we can find a way to change things. You don't have to be a prisoner anymore."

Rosie's eyes softened slightly, but the resentment was still there. "It's not that simple," she whispered. "There are things you don't understand, things that bind me to this chair. But if you truly want to help, you must be willing to face the darkness that holds me here."

"I gently picked her up and sat her down on the bed next to me" Is this better? I asked her. Her eyes went wide in shock and she froze, she wasn't expecting this.

"You are bold, I will give you that. No one has ever had the courage to touch me before. But what makes you think that sitting on a bed will make any difference? she said, her voice tinged with skepticism.

Then she realized she was able to move freely. Her eyes widened even more, and she looked at her hands, then back at me. "I… I can move," she whispered, almost in disbelief.

I nodded, trying to offer a reassuring smile. "Maybe this is a start.

Maybe we can figure out how to break whatever is binding you to that chair."

Rosie looked at me, a mix of hope and fear in her eyes. "You really think so?"

"I do," I replied. "But we'll need to work together. Can you tell me more about what happened to you? Maybe we can find a way to set you free."

She looked away for a moment, her expression softening. When she spoke again, her voice was quieter. "You are the first person to ask such a question. Most people just leave me sitting in my chair and dust me off every once in a while. Nobody has ever lifted me out of my chair."

She paused, tears starting to form in her eyes. Her dirty and dusty cheeks made the tears look even more poignant as they rolled down her face. "The reason I am confined to that rocking chair because…"

Her voice broke, and she struggled to continue. I reached out, gently placing a hand on her tiny shoulder. "It's okay, Rosie. Take your time. "When you are ready and feel like you can trust me, I am here for you."

I got off the bed and looked at her. "Rosie, this room is cold and eerie, and it's time you leave this room. Would you like to come to my room, feel better, and relax? You can explore around my room if you like." I extended my hand for her little hand.

Her eyes widened in surprise. She hesitantly took my hand, and I could feel her trembling slightly. Her voice was still quiet, but there was a hint of warmth in it. "I haven't left that room in years, and it would be nice to explore the real world again."

We went to my room and her eyes went wide seeing everything. She looking at all the posters of girls in bikinis and comic heroes and touching stuff on my shelves. I'm going to get a drink would you like a soda or a glass of water?

She stared at the wall of posters, her eyes darting back and forth from each one. She was speechless, clearly impressed by all the new things she had never seen before.

Turning to me, she stuttered, "Could I have a glass of water, please?"

"Okay, I'll be right back," I replied. I headed to the kitchen, where my grandma was napping in her easy chair. Quietly, I opened the fridge and grabbed a can of soda for myself. Then, I took an empty glass and made my way upstairs. I stopped by the bathroom to fill the glass with water before heading back to my room.

I walked into my room and she is sitting on my bed and I handed her the glass of water and she watches me pop my can open and she tilted her head, unsure what to make of it. I asked her if she would like to try taking a sip, its okay if you want to?

She hesitated for a moment, then gently took the can in her small hands. As she took a sip, her eyes lit up and a big grin spread across her face. “It’s good! I’ve never tasted something like this before.”

“I’ll be right back,” I said, quickly running back to the kitchen. Grandma was now at the sink, washing dishes. “Hi, Grandma!” I greeted her with a hug before grabbing another can of soda and dashing back upstairs to my room.

I entered my room, and she went to hand back the can of soda. “It’s okay, enjoy it,” I said, smiling. She smiled back, clearly enjoying her own can of soda.

“Thank you,” she said softly. “This is a nice experience.” Her happiness was evident, and I realized it must have been a long time since she had felt this way.

“You’re welcome, Rosie,” I said, still in disbelief that just hours ago, she had been a doll sitting in a rocker. I had no idea how long she had been left in that state. I got up and told her, “I’ll be right back.”

I ran to the bathroom, grabbed a washcloth, and filled a small tub with warm water and soap. Gently, I walked back to my room. She looked at me, her eyes widening in confusion as she saw the tub of water. “Why did you bring that here?” she asked, clearly puzzled.

I set the tub down on the floor and got down on my knees in front of her. Taking the wet washcloth, I tenderly took her small arm and gently began washing off the grime and years of dust. She watched me with wide eyes, a mix of curiosity and gratitude in her expression.

As I continued to clean her, I couldn’t help but wonder about the magic that had brought Her to life. How long had she been trapped in that form, and what had she seen and felt during all those years? The thought made me even more determined to help her experience the world anew.

Wiping off her little black shoes until they were shiny again, I then stood up and tenderly lifted her chin. She closed her eyes as I gently washed off her face and neck.

"Rosie, can you follow me back to the bathroom? I want to show you something in the mirror, and then you can decide what you want to do," I said softly.

She followed me back to the bathroom, and I helped her up onto a stool. As she looked into the mirror, tears began to well up in her eyes. Seeing herself so dusty and grimy from being forgotten for so many years was overwhelming.

I stood next to her, looking into the mirror as well. "I must admit, you do look amazing," I said softly. "You are a pretty girl now that I can see your clean face."

I was wondering now that you are able to move freely would you like to clean yourself up and would you like to (pointing to the tub) take a bath and I can take your outfit and go get them cleaned for you? Rosie looked at me, her eyes wide with a mix of surprise and gratitude. "A bath?" she repeated, as if the idea was foreign to her. She glanced at the tub, then back at me, her expression softening. "I… I would like that," she said quietly, a small smile forming on her lips.

She hesitated for a moment, then added, "Thank you for being so kind to me. It's been so long since anyone cared." Her voice trembled slightly, and I could see the emotions welling up inside her.

I smiled reassuringly. "It's my pleasure, Rosie. You deserve to feel clean and comfortable. I'll be right outside the door if you need anything. Just wrap yourself in a towel when you're done and hand me your outfit so I can put it with my dirty clothes and take them downstairs to be washed."

Rosie nodded, her eyes filled with gratitude. "Thank you," she whispered, her voice barely audible. She stepped into the bathroom, and I closed the door behind her, giving her some privacy.

As I waited outside, I couldn't help but think about how much her life had changed in such a short time. The thought of her finally experiencing simple joys like a bath made me smile. I wanted to make sure she felt safe and cared for in this new world she was discovering.

After a while, I heard the sound of water draining and soft footsteps approaching the door. Rosie opened it slightly, peeking out with a shy smile. She was wrapped in a towel, her hair damp and her face glowing from the warmth of the bath.

"Here," she said, handing me her outfit. "Thank you so much."

I took the clothes from her gently. "You're welcome, Rosie. I'll get these cleaned up for you. Feel free to use anything you need in the bathroom." She nodded, looking around the bathroom with a mix of curiosity and wonder. "It's all so new to me," she admitted, her voice soft.

I smiled. "Take your time. I'll be back with clean clothes."

After a while, I returned to the bathroom and gently knocked on the door. "Rosie, it's going to be a little while to wash and dry our clothes, so instead of you being in a towel and uncomfortable, I brought you a T-shirt and elastic shorts with a tie string. This way, you can move more freely."

Rosie opened the door slightly, peeking out with a curious expression. "Thank you," she said, taking the clothes from me. "I've never worn anything like this before."

I smiled reassuringly. "I think you'll find them comfortable. I'll be right outside if you need anything."

As she closed the door to change, I couldn't help but feel a sense of anticipation. Seeing Rosie adapt to her new surroundings and experiences was both heartwarming and fascinating. I wanted to make sure she felt as comfortable and welcome as possible in this new chapter of her life.

When she emerged from the bathroom, I almost fell over myself. I couldn't believe this was the same little girl I had found sitting in that rocker. She looked at me, sighed a little, and then quietly asked, "What is your name?"

I realized I had never introduced myself to her. Getting down on one knee, I held her hand like one would do for a princess and said, "I am Alex. It's my pleasure to meet you, Rosie."

Rosie smiled shyly, her eyes sparkling with curiosity. "Thank you, Alex," she said softly.

"I… I don't remember much about my past. It's all so hazy. But I feel safe with you."

I squeezed her hand gently. "I'm glad you feel that way, Rosie. We'll figure things out together. You don't have to worry about anything."

She looked around the room, taking in her new surroundings. "Everything is so different. It's like a whole new world."

I nodded. "It is. And there's so much for you to see and experience. We'll take it one step at a time."

Rosie hesitated for a moment, then asked, "Why did you help me? You didn't have to." I smiled, thinking back to the moment I found her. "When I saw you, I felt a connection. I couldn't just leave you there. Something inside me knew I had to help you."

Her eyes softened, and she took a deep breath. "Thank you, Alex. I don't know what I would have done without you."

As Rosie and I stood in my room, I realized that no one downstairs knew what had happened. My parents and grandma were completely unaware of the magical transformation that had taken place.

"Rosie," I said gently, "there's something you should know. This house belongs to my family, and my parents and grandma are downstairs. They don't know about you yet."

Rosie looked at me with wide eyes. "What should we do?"

I thought for a moment. "First, let's get you settled. Then, we'll figure out how to introduce you to my family. They might be surprised, but I think they'll understand once we explain everything."

Rosie nodded, her expression a mix of nervousness and excitement. "Okay. But… what if they don't believe us?"

I smiled reassuringly. "We'll take it one step at a time. For now, let's focus on getting you comfortable."

As we talked, I couldn't help but think about my great aunt. Rosie had once been her doll, and there had to be a reason why she was cursed. Maybe my grandma knew something about it. She had always been the keeper of family stories and secrets.

"Rosie," I said, "do you remember anything about my great aunt? Anything at all?"

Rosie furrowed her brow, trying to recall. "I remember… she was kind to me. She used to tell me stories and sing lullabies. But then, one day, everything changed. I don't know why."

I nodded, feeling a sense of determination. "We'll figure it out together. Maybe my grandma can help us. She knows a lot about our family's history."

Rosie smiled, a glimmer of hope in her eyes. "Thank you, Alex. I don't feel so alone anymore."

I squeezed her hand gently. "You're not alone, Rosie. We'll uncover the truth and make sure you have a chance to live your life as it should have been."

After making sure Rosie was comfortable, I decided it was time to talk to my grandma. She had always been the keeper of our family's stories and secrets, and I hoped she might know something about Rosie's past.

"Rosie, let's go talk to my grandma," I said. "She might be able to help us understand what happened to you."

Rosie nodded, a mix of curiosity and nervousness in her eyes. "Okay."

We made our way downstairs, and I found my grandma in the living room, knitting in her favorite chair. She looked up and smiled when she saw us.

"Hi, Grandma," I said, giving her a hug. "There's someone I want you to meet."

Grandma's eyes twinkled with curiosity as she looked at Rosie. "And who is this lovely young lady?"

"This is Rosie," I said, gently guiding Rosie forward. "She used to be Aunt Clara's doll."

Grandma's smile froze, her knitting needles pausing mid-stitch. "Aunt Clara's doll?" she repeated, her voice barely above a whisper. "But how…?"

"It's a long story," I said, sitting down next to her. "Rosie was cursed and turned into a doll for many years. Today, she came back to life."

Grandma looked at Rosie with a mixture of awe and concern. "Oh, my dear. You've been through so much."

Rosie nodded, her voice barely above a whisper. "I don't remember much, but I know Aunt Clara was kind to me. Then one day, everything changed."

Grandma sighed, her expression thoughtful. "Aunt Clara was a wonderful woman, but she had her secrets. There were rumors about her dabbling in magic, but I never believed them. Perhaps there was more truth to those stories than I realized."

"Do you know anything about the curse?" I asked.

Grandma shook her head. "I'm afraid I don't. But I do remember Aunt Clara mentioning a special book she kept hidden. She said it contained powerful spells and secrets. Maybe that book holds the answers we're looking for."

"Where is it?" Rosie asked, her eyes wide with hope.

Grandma smiled gently. "It's in the attic, hidden in a chest. I'll show you."

We followed Grandma up to the attic, the air thick with dust and memories. She led us to an old wooden chest and carefully opened it. Inside, among various trinkets and keepsakes, was a worn, leather-bound book.

"This is it," Grandma said, handing the book to me. "Be careful with it. It's very old and very powerful."

I took the book, feeling a sense of anticipation. "Thank you, Grandma. We'll be careful."

As we made our way back downstairs, I couldn't help but feel a sense of excitement. We were one step closer to uncovering the truth about Rosie's past and breaking the curse for good.

Back in my room, Rosie and I sat down with the worn, leather-bound book on the bed between us. The cover was faded, and the pages were yellowed with age. I carefully opened it, revealing intricate illustrations and handwritten notes in the margins.

"This is incredible," I whispered, feeling the weight of the book's history. Rosie leaned in closer, her eyes wide with curiosity. "What does it say?"

I began to read aloud, translating the old-fashioned script. "It looks like this book contains powerful spells and secrets. There are instructions on how to create magical objects, perform spells, and even summon supernatural entities."

Rosie shivered slightly. "Do you think there's something in here about my curse?"

I nodded. "Let's keep looking. There must be something."

As we turned the pages, we found a section titled "Curses and Transformations." My heart raced as I read through the descriptions. Finally, we came across a passage that seemed relevant:

"To reverse a curse of transformation, one must find the object of the curse and perform a ritual of cleansing and renewal. The ritual requires the following ingredients: a personal item of the cursed, a symbol of purity, and a token of love."

Rosie looked at me, her eyes filled with hope. "Do you think we can do it?"

I smiled reassuringly. "I think we can. We just need to gather the ingredients and perform the ritual."

We spent the next few hours searching through the book for more details about the ritual. It was clear that Aunt Clara had been involved in powerful magic, and this book was a testament to her knowledge and skills.

"Rosie," I said, "do you have any personal items from before you were cursed?"

She thought for a moment, then nodded. "I think there's a locket in the attic. Aunt Clara gave it to me. It was very special to her."

"Perfect," I said. "We'll need that for the ritual. Now, we just need to find a symbol of purity and a token of love."

Rosie smiled, a glimmer of determination in her eyes. "Let's do it, Alex. Let's break this curse once and for all."

Rosie and I made our way to the attic, the wooden stairs creaking under our weight. The air grew colder as we ascended, and a sense of anticipation filled the space between us.

The attic was cluttered with old furniture, dusty boxes, and forgotten memories. Rosie led the way, her eyes scanning the room until they landed on a small, ornate box tucked away in a corner.

She carefully opened the box and retrieved the locket. It was a delicate piece, with intricate engravings and a small, faded photograph inside. Rosie held it close, her fingers trembling slightly.

"This locket was Aunt Clara's most cherished possession," she said softly. "She always told me it held the key to our family's legacy."

I nodded, feeling the weight of the moment. "Now we need to find a symbol of purity and a token of love. Any ideas?"

Rosie thought for a moment, then her face lit up. "There's a white rose bush in the garden. Aunt Clara planted it herself. It always blooms, no matter the season. And for the token of love…I have a letter my mother wrote to my father before they were married. It's filled with so much love and hope."

"That sounds perfect," I said. "Let's gather everything and prepare for the ritual."

As we descended the stairs, I couldn't help but feel a sense of hope. We were one step closer to breaking the curse and freeing Rosie from its grasp. Together, we would face whatever challenges lay ahead.

With the locket, the white rose, and the love letter in hand, we stood in the center of the room, ready to begin the ritual. The air was thick with anticipation, and the flickering candlelight cast dancing shadows on the walls.

"Are you ready, Rosie?" I asked, my voice barely above a whisper.

She nodded, her eyes filled with determination and a hint of fear. "Yes, Alex. Let's do this."

We began chanting the ancient words from Aunt Clara's book, our voices blending together in a harmonious rhythm. As the incantation grew more intense, I could feel the magic swirling around us, a palpable force that seemed to pulse with our every word.

When the final words of the chant left our lips, I looked into Rosie's eyes, seeing the depth of her soul reflected back at me. Without thinking, I leaned in and kissed her tenderly, our lips meeting in a moment of pure connection. The items we held in our hands seemed to glow with an inner light, as if responding to the power of our love.

As we pulled away, a soft, shimmering light enveloped Rosie, lifting the curse that had bound her for so long. Tears of relief and joy streamed down her face, and I knew that we had succeeded.

"Thank you, Alex," she whispered, her voice choked with emotion. "I couldn't have done this without you."

I smiled, wiping away her tears. "We'll always be together, Rosie. No curse can ever change that."

Rosie and I descended the stairs, our faces beaming with excitement and relief. As we entered the living room, we found Grandma sitting with my parents, their expressions a mix of curiosity and concern.

"What's going on?" my mother asked, her eyes darting between Rosie and me.

Grandma smiled warmly, her eyes twinkling with pride. "It's a long story, but I think it's best if Rosie and Alex explain."

Rosie took a deep breath and stepped forward, her voice steady but filled with emotion.

"Mom, Dad, we've been working on breaking the curse that Aunt Clara placed on me. With Alex's help, we found the necessary items and performed the ritual."

My father's eyebrows shot up in surprise. "A curse? Ritual? What are you talking about?"

I stepped in, placing a reassuring hand on Rosie's shoulder. "It's true. Aunt Clara was involved in powerful magic, and Rosie was cursed. But we did it—we broke the curse together."

My parents exchanged glances, processing the information. Finally, my mother spoke, her voice softening. "Is it really over? Are you okay, Rosie?"

Rosie nodded, tears of joy welling up in her eyes. "Yes, it's over. I feel free for the first time in years."

A wave of relief washed over the room, and my parents rushed to embrace Rosie. Grandma watched with a satisfied smile, knowing that the family's bond had grown even stronger through this ordeal.

As we all sat down together, the weight of the past few hours began to lift, replaced by a sense of hope and unity. We had faced the unknown and emerged victorious, and now, we could look forward to a future filled with love and possibility.

As we sat together, the reality of Rosie's situation began to sink in. She was still a young girl from the past, and we needed to find a way to integrate her into our family without raising suspicion.

"Rosie," I said gently, "we need to figure out how to explain your presence here. We can't let anyone find out the real truth."

Grandma nodded thoughtfully. "We could say she's a distant relative who has come to live with us. That would explain why she's staying here and why she might not know much about modern things."

My mother looked at Rosie with a kind smile. "We can help you adjust to this time. We'll teach you everything you need to know, and you'll be part of our family."

Rosie smiled, her eyes shining with gratitude. "Thank you. I promise I'll do my best to fit in."

My father chimed in, "We'll need to get some documents in order. Birth certificate, school records… I'll make some calls and see what we can do."

Over the next few days, we worked together to create a new identity for Rosie. We enrolled her in school, explaining to the staff that she was a relative who had come to live with us after a family tragedy. Rosie adapted quickly, her natural curiosity and intelligence helping her navigate the modern world.

At home, we shared stories and laughter, growing closer as a family. Rosie became a beloved member of our household, her past a secret we all vowed to protect. Together, we faced the challenges of blending the old with the new, knowing that our love and unity would see us through.

That evening, Rosie and I sat on the back porch, the cool night air wrapping around us like a comforting blanket. The sky was clear, the moon casting a gentle glow over the landscape, and the stars twinkling like distant diamonds.

I took Rosie's hand in mine, feeling the warmth of her touch. "Rosie," I began softly, "I love you so much. I feel truly blessed to be your savior, and I look forward to our future together as we grow older."

She smiled, her eyes reflecting the moonlight, and rested her head on my shoulder. “I love you too, Alex,” she whispered, her voice filled with emotion. She held my hand tightly, and we embraced each other, finding comfort and strength in our connection.

Together, we gazed up at the moon and stars, feeling a sense of peace and hope for the future. In that moment, everything felt right, and we knew that no matter what challenges lay ahead, we would face them together.

The End

The Orphanage Child

Nova

Chapter 1
Nova

NOVA SITS QUIETLY in the corner of the playground, her blonde hair falling over her face as she fixes the frilly dress on her favorite doll. She glances up shyly at the other loud, energetic kids running and shouting nearby, but quickly looks back down, hugging her doll tighter. Her pacifier bobs rhythmically in her mouth as she makes her doll dance and twirl on the ground.

"Muu..." She whimpers softly, wishing she could work up the courage to ask the other children if she can join their game. But her shyness overwhelms her, so she continues playing alone. The doll's silly antics make her giggle behind her pacifier, the laughter lighting up her big, round eyes.For now, her beloved doll is the only playmate she needs.

Nova resumes dressing up her toy, dreaming of the day she'll finally step out of her loneliness and find a real friend and family. Seeing her and holding these papers I walked up to her , The other kids just watched me, it got very quiet outside and everyone was watching. I got down in front of Nova and spoke to her) Hello Nova remember me? (I visit her a few months ago at the Orphanage but I had to get a DNA test to prove I was her legal parent) Nova perks up when she sees me. "Ken...neth-kun?" Her eyes light up, and she hugs her doll tighter against her chest. "Mm. Hi." She nods slowly, still shy but visibly happy to see him. Nova had often talked about Kenneth visiting her dreams, and sometimes, when she was bored or lonely, she pretended that he was her friend. He seemed so kind and gentle

—someone she could trust with her big, round eyes full of innocence and hope.

Nova looks up at him uncertainly as he speaks again. "I... um, I don't know, mister." She frowns, her big pink eyes welling up with tears. Suddenly, she remembers everything he told her when they first met at the orphanage. Her mom's death, her abandonment by everyone else, she was afraid to hope that he was real, that he would never leave her like everyone else. Still holding onto her doll, she moves closer to him, taking small steps forward while sucking softly on her pacifier.

Nova, how would you like to come home with me? And be my darling little daughter as it should have been? All the other kids stood and stared, some even had tears falling from their faces they knew what was happening. Nova was being Adopted and has a home to go to. Nova's eyes grow wider as Kenneth speaks. Her breath hitches, and she chews on her bottom lip. Would this be real? Was Kenneth finally going to take her away from the loneliness and the sorrow of her past? She nods rapidly. "Yes! Yes, please." Her voice is soft, almost a whisper, but the urgency in her eyes speaks volumes. Reaching out tentatively with her free hand, she grabs onto my sleeve, holding onto me with all her might.

A momentary flash of sadness flickers across her face as she remembers her mother's tears and words, when she told her about Kenneth at the orphanage, That he was her real father. She wondered how will he find her. Would they ever be reunited? For now, though, Nova lets the hope blossom inside her as she follows Kenneth willingly, leaving behind the old, tattered dress she was patching up for her doll. Maybe in this new home, she would finally make a real friend someone who'd never leave her. Holding onto her precious, well-loved pacifier, she takes a tentative step towards a brighter future with every stride.

Still the other kids didn.t say anything, most just fell on their knees crying happy tears for Nova, They all waved good-by as we drove away and Nova looking out the window, looking at the building and the others and thanking God for saving her. The ride to Kenneth's home was long and quiet. Nova was still a bit nervous about leaving her familiar surroundings, but she trusted that he would take care of her. Her heart swelled with joy when he handed her a stuffed animal he brought for her on the way home, telling her it was from her 'new family'.

The ride seemed shorter when they played games and talked softly to each other. As they arrived at their new house, Kenneth guided Nova inside. He introduced her to his wife and daughter who would be Nova's older sister, "Her protector." all smiling warmly at their newest member. Nova felt a rush of emotion as she saw their happiness spreading like wildfire—they seemed so content together, and they welcomed her into their family with open arms. The sadness of losing her mother and fearing being left alone faded into the background; for now, all she felt was love and hope.

Well dear what do you think ,can we make this our lovely home Nova? Nova nodded eagerly, her big pink eyes shining with anticipation. "Yes, Ken...neth-kun. This is a beautiful home." She looked around, taking in the cozy living room, the colorful paintings on the wall, and the warm light filtering in through the windows. For the first time in a long time, Nova felt like she belonged somewhere. She hugged her new stuffed animal tightly, feeling its soft fur against her cheek. "Thank you, Ken...neth-kun. I'm so happy to be here with you.

"Her voice was small but filled with gratitude. As they explored their new home together, Nova couldn't help but wonder what adventures awaited her in this new chapter of her life. But for now, she was content to cuddle up on the couch with her new sister and a mommy and daddy and watch cartoons while sucking on her pacifier—a simple pleasure that felt like heaven after years of loneliness.

Chapter 2
First Night

OK KIDS. Time for dinner then bath, then cuddle and then bed time. "Muu..." Nova nodded eagerly, her eyes sparkling with excitement. She followed Kenneth obediently, her heart pounding with anticipation.

Dinner was delicious—spaghetti and meatballs, her favorite!—and they laughed and chatted throughout the meal.After dinner, it was bath time. Kenneth's wife helped her undress and carefully washed her body, being extra gentle with the still-healing scars on her legs from her fall down the stairs, they said she did at the orphanage. She hummed softly to calm her nerves, and Nova couldn't help but feel safe and loved in her arms.

As they cuddled on the couch after her bath, watching TV together, Nova slipped her pacifier out of her mouth for the first time since Kenneth found her. She felt more secure and happy than she had in years, finally free from the burden of her fear and loneliness.

Looking up at Kenneth with big, round eyes full of trust, she whispered softly, "Thank you, Ken...neth-kun." And with that, she drifted off to sleep in his arms, dreaming of a bright future filled with love and laughter.

Slowly I picked her up in my arms and brought her to her bed and gently laid her down, I slipped off her slippers and covered her with a blanket and stuffed her new toy in her arms. I bent down and kissed her cheek.

"Good Night my child ,Daddy loves you" I went to the other side of the bed, sat on the bed and watched over her, (figured since this is all new to her different sounds, no other kids coughing or crying in their sleep, I didn't want her to wake up frighten) Nova woke up slightly startled, her eyes widening as she realized where she was and who was beside her. She had never slept in a bed this big, surrounded by soft blankets and cuddly toys. Kenneth was there too, Seems while sitting against her head board he fell asleep sitting up. Despite being a bit disoriented at first, Nova felt oddly safe and happy having me close by her. She snuggled closer to him,and hugged him, her soft breathing calming down. For the first time in a long time, she fell back asleep peacefully, secure in the knowledge that she wasn't alone anymore.-I sat there thinking about what she gone thru and the pain and sadness, I started tearing up, and being left at a place like that. I don't know who sent me a telegram telling me I had a daughter, and she needed me to come, and where she was. It took a while to get legal papers stating she was my daughter and I was her legal parent. Slowly I also fell asleep sitting up beside my darling daughter-Nova slept soundly throughout the night, her small body nestled against Kenneth's chest. She didn't stir even once, her breathing steady and peaceful. Kenneth held her close, his heart swelling with love and protectiveness for this precious little girl who had been through so much.As the sun began to peek through the curtains, Kenneth gently disentangled himself from Nova's sleeping form. He tucked her in more snugly, kissed her forehead, and whispered, "Good morning, my dear. Daddy's here." He then quietly got off the bed, leaving Nova to wake up at her own pace.

When Nova finally opened her eyes, she blinked blearily, taking in her new surroundings. She smiled softly, feeling a warmth spread through her chest. This was home. This was where I belonged. And with my daddy by my side, she knew that she would never be alone again she now has a family. -I walked into the room she was awake but still bundle up, she sees me and sits up and I sat next to her- . Darling I know this is all new to you and you went through really bad times but that's in the past. I am very lucky someone told me about you, its why they had to come and take samples from you. For me to prove I am your real daddy you are my blood.

Me and your mom gave you life, but if I knew I had a daughter you would have never been in that kind of place or have the life you went though.

Nova nodded, her big pink eyes welling up with tears. She sniffled and wiped her nose with her arm, trying to hold back the tears. Kenneth gently wrapped his arms around her, pulling her close. "Shh... it's okay, sweetheart. Daddy's here now, and we're going to take care of you from now on, okay?"Nova nodded again, this time burying her face in Kenneth's chest. She let out a shaky breath and said "daddy", her body trembling slightly.

Kenneth held her tightly, stroking her hair and whispering soothing words to calm her down. After a few minutes, Nova's breathing slowed down. He kissed her forehead gently, his heart filled with love and gratitude for this precious little girl who had found her way into his life. He knew it wouldn't be easy, but he was ready to do whatever it took to make sure Nova was happy and safe.(I hope she keeps calling me daddy, just heard her say it once warmed my hearth and soul. I have my daughter and will do what ever to protect her and love her) Nova blinked, looking up at Kenneth with big, curious eyes. "What do you mean, Daddy?"

She asked innocently, her pacifier still in her mouth."Well, sweetheart, it's just that... hearing you call me 'daddy' makes me really happy. It's a special word between parents and their children, you know?" Kenneth explained, smiling gently at her.Nova tilted her head to the side, thinking about what Kenneth had said. "Oh," she replied simply, before nodding and burying her face back into Kenneth's chest. "Daddy."

Kenneth chuckled softly, his heart filled with love for this little girl who had found her way into his life. "That's my girl," he whispered, kissing the top of her head. "Always remember that I'm here for you, Nova" The rest of the family walked in and we all got on the bed a hugged out little addition.we are a total family now.As Nova clings to it, perhaps it becomes her silent confidante, soaking up her whispered secrets and fears.

In the quiet moments, when the world feels too big, Kenneth watches her with a tender smile. He knows that the binkie isn’t just a piece of fabric; it’s a lifeline connecting Nova to safety, to love, and to the promise that she belongs. And so, in the warmth of their newfound family, the binkie remains—a steadfast companion.

Chapter 3
Nova's Binkie

ITS SUMMER and we all gathered up things to head to the beach, Something Nova never seen before or had the opportunity to ever witness. As we drove along the road along the beautiful beach the kids was cheering on but little Nove just looking and sucking on her Binkie with wide eyes.

The sun hung high in the sky, its golden rays dancing upon the azure waves. Ourfamily—Ken, the kids, and little Nova—packed the car with beach towels, sandcastle buckets, and a picnic basket filled with laughter. It was a day of firsts, especially for Nova.

As we drove along the winding coastal road, the kids pressed their faces against the windows, their excitement contagious. They chattered about building sandcastles, collecting seashells, and chasing seagulls. But Nova sat quietly in her car seat, clutching her binkie, eyes wide like saucers.

"Look, Nova!" Lily, the eldest, pointed. "See the ocean? It's like a giant blue blanket!"

Nova blinked, taking it all in—the vast expanse of water stretching to infinity. She'd never seen anything like it—the rhythmic ebb and flow, the salty breeze that tousled her hair. Her binkie remained steadfast, a tiny anchor in this new world.

"Is it magic?" Nova whispered, her voice barely audible. Ken glanced at her through the rearview mirror, his heart swelling. “Yes, my love. It’s a kind of magic.”

We parked near the dunes, and Nova stepped onto the warm sand. The grains clung to her tiny toes, and she wobbled, giggling. The kids raced toward the water, their laughter carried by the wind. Nova hesitated, then followed, her binkie dangling from her lips. The waves lapped at her ankles, and Nova squealed. “It’s like a giant bath, Daddy!

"Ken scooped her up, twirling her around. “And you’re the mermaid, Nova.” She grinned, her eyes reflecting the cerulean sea. “Mermaid Nova,” she declared. As the day unfolded, Nova built her first sandcastle—a lopsided masterpiece adorned with seashells and seaweed. She tasted salt-water, felt the sun kiss her cheeks, and discovered that seagulls were cheeky thieves. Her binkie lay forgotten in the sand, a testament to newfound wonder.

When the sun dipped low, casting a golden path across the water, Nova nestled into Ken’s arms. The kids gathered seashells, their pockets overflowing. Nova traced her finger along the horizon, where the sky met the sea.

“Daddy,” she said, her voice soft, “is this forever?” Ken hugged her tight. “As long as you want it to be, Nova.” And so, on that sun-kissed beach, Nova’s heart expanded—a tiny universe of sand, salt, and love.

The sun dipped low on the horizon, casting a warm glow across the sandy shore. Nova stood there, her tiny fingers tracing the edges of her binkie—the soft fabric worn from countless nights of whispered dreams and secret adventures.

Kenneth watched from a distance, his heart swelling with pride. His little girl had come so far—the orphaned child who clung to that binkie like a lifeline. But now, something had shifted. Nova’s eyes, wide and curious, scanned the horizon. She no longer needed the binkie to anchor her.

“Daddy,” she said, her voice small but resolute, “I think it’s time.” He knelt beside her, the waves lapping at their toes. “Time for what, my love?” Nova hesitated, then held out the binkie. “I don’t need this anymore. I have you and I have a family.”

Tears blurred Kenneth’s vision as he took the binkie. He tucked it into his pocket—a reminder of resilience, of love found in unexpected places. And together, hand in hand, they walked away from the shore, leaving behind the past and stepping into a future where family was their greatest treasure.

🎂🎉 Happy birthday, Nova! 🎁🎈

The air buzzed with anticipation as Nova's siblings exchanged secretive glances. They'd been plotting something special, and Nova, her wide eyes filled with curiosity, had no inkling of the surprise awaiting her. In the cozy kitchen, Ken stirred pancake batter, a mischievous grin tugging at his lips.

"Nova," he said, "today is your day. Any guesses?"

Nova shook her head, her binkie dangling from her mouth. "Is it a treasure hunt?"

Lily, the eldest, winked. "Not quite, little mermaid."

As the morning sun streamed through the window, Nova's siblings led her outside. The backyard had transformed—a kaleidoscope of colors. Balloons bobbed in the breeze, and a banner proclaimed, "Happy 6th Birthday, Nova!"

Nova gasped. "For me? "For you," Lily confirmed. "And there's more."

They guided her to a table laden with treats: cupcakes crowned with star-shaped sprinkles, a tower of pancakes drizzled with maple syrup, and a fruit salad bursting with rainbows. Nova's eyes widened, and she clapped her hands.

"Breakfast feast!" she declared. But that wasn't all. Ken handed her a small box. Inside, nestled like a secret, was a seashell necklace—the kind mermaids wore, he explained. Nova beamed, slipping it around her neck.

"Thank you, Daddy," she whispered. As the day unfolded, Nova danced in the grass, her binkie forgotten for once. She blew out candles, her wish a secret shared only with the wind. And when the sun dipped low, casting a golden glow, the family gathered around Nova.

"Make a wish," Lily said. Nova closed her eyes, her heart full. She wished for endless summers, sandcastles, and love that stretched wider than the ocean. And as the stars blinked into existence, Nova knew—this was her magic day. A day of family, laughter, and the promise that she belonged.

Chapter 4
Meeting Grandma and Grandpa

THERES A KNOCK on the front door, Nova saw Lily Running to the door yelling "Their here Their here" Nova looking out the window Of her bedroom and sees two older people outside and her siblings hugging and getting kisses, she starts to get withdrawn, "Who are these people she is thinking?"

Ah, the arrival of Grandma and Grandpa—a moment both exciting and bewildering for young Nova. As she peers through the window, her little heart flutters with questions. Who are these strangers, and why do her siblings embrace them so tightly? The older couple stands there, their faces etched with years of stories. Grandma's eyes crinkle at the corners, and Grandpa's hands tremble slightly. They carry a suitcase—their journey to this doorstep a tapestry of memories.

Nova hesitates. She's the observer—the quiet star in this family constellation. But as Lily pulls her toward the door, Nova takes a deep breath. Maybe, just maybe, these strangers hold secrets—the kind that unravel into love.

And so, as the door swings open, Nova steps into their embrace. Grandma's perfume—a hint of lavender—wraps around her. Grandpa's voice, gravelly and kind, whispers, "Hello, little one." In that moment, Nova begins a new chapter—the one where strangers become kin, and love becomes a language spoken across generations.

Grandma stayed indoors helping my mom making dinner, Daddy and Lily are setting up the dining room and Grandpa grabs my little hand and we walk outside to the back porch and he picked me up at put me on the porch swing and sat next to me.

The weathered porch swing, creaking as we sat together, I sit there, wide-eyed, as he recounts adventures. He tells me about the oak tree in the backyard—the one that witnessed his childhood escapades. How he climbed its branches, scraped his knees, and dreamed of distant lands. I listen, my little heart a compass pointing toward wonder.

Your grandfather's eyes crinkle when he laughs. His hands, calloused from years of toil, gesture toward the horizon. "Remember," he says, "we're part of something bigger and we are very happy you came into our lives little one." He hugged me and I hugged him back.

In the heart of the house, Grandma's kitchen hummed with life. The stove crackled, pots clanged, and spices danced in harmony. She wore an apron—the fabric a canvas of love stains and secret recipes. Mommy and Grandma, sleeves rolled up, coaxing flavors from humble ingredients. The scent of simmering soup or freshly baked bread wafted through the air. And as the clock ticked toward dinner, anticipation grew.

Mommy and Grandma came outside to let us know it was dinner time, I reached up and Grandpa lifted me up in his arms and carried me inside. Daddy and Lily had everything ready The dining room table stood proud—a witness to countless stories. Its polished surface reflected faces—wrinkled, youthful, and everything in between. The chairs creaked as everyone settled in—the clatter of cutlery, the rustle of napkins.

And then, the ritual began. Heads bowed, hands clasped, hearts open. Grace flowed—a whispered thank you for sustenance, for togetherness, for the simple joy of being alive. Grandma's eyes sparkled as she led the chorus. Platters appeared—laden with memories. Roast chicken, golden and succulent. Mashed potatoes, creamy as Grandma's laughter. Green beans, crisp and vibrant. And always, a warm loaf of bread—the heartbeat of the meal.Conversations swirled—a symphony of voices.

Laughter bubbled like a brook. Stories emerged—Daddy told the time Uncle Joe spilled gravy, the secret ingredient in Aunt Mary's pie. And

Grandma, at the head of the table, beamed. This was something I was never seen before even at the Orphanage , we always had to eat in quiet, This was so much nicer.

Dessert arrived—a sweet crescendo. Apple pie, its crust flaky as promises kept. Ice cream scoops piled high. As forks scraped plates, you'd catch her eye. She'd wink—a silent acknowledgment of shared joy. And in that moment, the dining room expanded—a universe of love, laughter, and belonging. Then the surprise was brought out with candles burning, Since they couldn't be there on my day today they wanted to give me another Birthday. Grandpa brought out Grandma's famous chocolate cake—the one that made birthdays magical. And it surely was magical for me and getting to meet my grandparents. After we ate and everyone pitch in even me we cleaned up the kitchen and dining room. Then we all went back outside on the back porch and there was a few boxes , I looked at them and saw my name on some and Lily's , The ones to me was for my birthday presents from grandma and grandpa and so Lily wouldn't feel left out they brought her some to open too.

Also by Kenneth Haines

A Tale of Escape

A group of Earthlings, including a young woman named Elara, is abducted by an invisible alien ship to become part of a cosmic exhibition. Facing the reality of being observed by an alien audience, they form a bond and ignite a longing for freedom. Together, they plot their escape, daring to dream of returning to their lives on Earth. As they navigate their captivity and fight for autonomy, they are tested but remain unbroken, driven by the hope of weaving their experiences back into humanity's story.

* * *

Whispers in the Sand

Amidst the whispers of the sand and the caress of the Autumn sea, a tale of survival unfolds on the shores of a forsaken island. Here, young Selene and her father carve out an existence, relying on the embrace of nature and each other. Their bond, once threatened by tragedy, burgeons under the trials they face in this barren refuge. But when the island yields an unexpected reunion, the fabric of their family is woven together once more, painting a poignant portrait of hope and resilience. In the cool embrace of a late afternoon's breeze, Selene's heart finds solace, and together, they etch a new beginning upon their souls—an indelible whisper in the fabric of time.

* * *

Tylorin

In the oppressive kingdom of Eldaf, where elves endure human cruelty, a desperate elf mother and her child find an unexpected ally in a compassionate human. Together, they embark on a perilous escape through secret paths and natural sanctuaries, aided by the whispers of the forest's denizens. Their journey leads them to an abandoned, tranquil cottage, where they begin a new life of resilience and love. United by courage and kinship, their bond transcends blood, offering hope and peace amidst the shadows of their past.

Echoes of Laughter, Echoes of Fear

In an abandoned amusement park reclaimed by nature, five young explorersâ€”three girls and two boysâ€”embark on an adventure filled with mystery and spectral intrigue. Amid peeling paint and rusting rides, they delve into the park's hidden sorrows, blending nostalgia with a sense of foreboding. As they confront both the park's secrets and their own fears, their journey becomes a test of courage, friendship, and the human spirit. In this eerie yet captivating odyssey, the line between joy and darkness blurs, leaving them to discover whether their bonds can light the way through the park's enigmatic shadows.

* * *

Sea of Shadows

Stranded on a solitary island, young Helene navigates a journey of survival and self-discovery, guided by the wisdom of her late father and the lessons of the untamed wilderness. Amid the island's deceptive tranquility, she transforms grief into resilience, building a sanctuary from remnants of the past and forging a future shaped by love and fortitude. Through hardship, Helene finds strength in enduring connections, her father's presence ever a guiding light. Her odyssey is one of emotional catharsis and renewal, where each dawn heralds the triumph of hope and the radiance of new beginnings.

Enchanted Citadel

In a realm where magic and technology intertwine, a group of elite space voyagers embarks on a perilous quest to recover the Chrono Crystal, an ancient gemstone vital for stabilizing the magical streams of their soaring sanctuary, the Enchanted Citadel. As they traverse vibrant yet conflicted planets, they face arcane guardians and looming threats of a malevolent siege. Amidst a cosmic battlefield where starships glide on waves of sorcery and science, the voyagers grapple with unity and betrayal, illuminating paths once hidden in the shadows.

* * *

Time has stopped

In *Time Has Stopped*, Elara and her band of weary travelers navigate an endless red desert, a harsh landscape that was once ruled by oceans and now conceals the secrets of a long-lost, water-bound civilization. Battling scorching heat, deceptive mirages, and unforgiving storms, their journey leads them to a colossal statue and an underground labyrinth echoing with the remnants of a forgotten world. Along the way, they form an unlikely bond with a mysterious creature whose loyalty may be their only hope for survival. As the desert tests their resilience and courage, each step comes with sacrifice, forcing them to confront how far they are willing to go to survive the relentless sands of time.

* * *

Starborn

In a distant cosmos, the crew of a valiant starship embarks on a perilous journey through the galactic veil, uncovering relics of the ancient Starborn civilizationâ€”artifacts of immense power and potential ruin. As they navigate celestial ruins and decipher esoteric transmissions, the explorers grapple with internal tensions and looming cosmic adversaries. Each discovery brings them closer to revolutionary breakthroughs while risking catastrophic consequences. Caught between enlightenment and oblivion, their odyssey becomes a profound reflection on the morality of progress and the price of knowledge, weaving a tale of human resolve amidst the vast, enigmatic expanse of the stars.

* * *

Tales of the Unknown

Word in the forest was that something wasn't right and the creatures were on edge and the slightest noise or movement made them run for cover. Word of this came to Sanction while he was foliage for food. A wagon rolled up and tossed a young girl child from it, she was wrapped inside a burlap potato bag and was tossed aside like trash. Child please dry them tears for you are safe in my forest, like I said no harm will come to you. She sits up and listens to his every word.

Jake found himself enjoying the solitude of the open road. That is, until his car started to sputter. A sudden jolt, leaving Jake stranded in the middle of nowhere. Desperate for help, Jake decided to head towards the building, hoping to find a phone or someone who could assist. Soon to find he has entered where time had stopped and the souls of who where left behind needed to be saved.

* * *

Whispers in the Sand

Amidst the whispers of the sand and the caress of the Autumn sea, a tale of survival unfolds on the shores of a forsaken island. Here, young Selene and her father carve out an existence, relying on the embrace of nature and each other. Their bond, once threatened by tragedy, burgeons under the trials they face in this barren refuge. But when the island yields an unexpected reunion, the fabric of their family is woven together once more, painting a poignant portrait of hope and resilience. In the cool embrace of a late afternoon's breeze, Selene's heart finds solace, and together, they etch a new beginning upon their souls—an indelible whisper in the fabric of time.

www.ingramcontent.com/pod-product-compliance
Lightning Source LLC
LaVergne TN
LVHW010503160826
845677LV00012B/2629